P9-BYY-815

Max, Mollie, and the Magic of Sea Glass

A Lesson in Character

By Ardis Glace

Copyright © 2015

All rights reserved. No part of this book may be reproduced
in any form without written permission from the author and illustrator.

ISBN: 978-0-9862655-0-1
2nd printing

Author: Ardis A. Glace
Designer: Erin VanWerden
Illustrator: Cindy Nuygen; Gau Family Studios

Publisher: Creative Impact, Des Moines, Iowa

A Little About Lily

The real Lily is a wonderful woman who lives in Mexico and has been tumbled
more in life than one can imagine. Yet, after years of hardship and heartbreak
she continues living life with a smile and determination to survive. Because Lily
was born and raised in Mexico City and then lived in North America for more
than 20 years she has created some expressions and word usage that are a
little unusual. You might notice these phrases throughout the book. These are
expressions that she uses in her every day speech. Lily's Mexican/English dialect
is sprinkled with numerous word combinations that make us smile.

Max and Mollie love going to the beach.
Every time they visit they discover something new.

One beautiful summer day Max and Mollie were looking for shells on the beach when they saw a bright and sparkling rock at the edge of the water. Just as they reached for it a wave crashed in and pulled it back out to sea.

Soon Mollie found another sparkly rock and grabbed it before it could disappear. "Max, LOOK I got one! I think it might be a HUGE diamond!"

"Over here," Max called. "I found a blue one that's even bigger than your diamond—it's GIGANTIC!"

"Where do you think these came from?" Mollie asked her twin brother.

"I think they are from a pirate ship!" he said.

"Or maybe they are magic," Mollie added.

"HA!" laughed Max. "Maybe they are magic rocks buried by the pirates!"

Later that day, Max and Mollie showed the jewels to their grandfather.

"Are we going to be rich?" Max asked.

"I don't know about that," Granddad laughed. "If you look closely you can see these are just pieces of broken glass that washed on to the shore. You can throw them away or keep them in your treasure box."

Max couldn't believe what he was hearing. "They can't be trash! Broken glass is sharp and jagged. I stepped on a piece once and it cut my foot. These are WAY too smooth."

"Sorry Max," Granddad sighed as he gave both a hug. "No diamonds or rubies here. Just sea glass that washed on to the beach."

That night neither twin could fall asleep. Mollie read a
book while Max rubbed the smooth blue glass in his hand.
"I WISH this was something magic," he said.

"Please be quiet Max. I'm reading."

"I WISH this was a magic ROCK!"

"SHHH. Max, be quiet."

"I WISH THIS WAS A MAGIC ROCK!!"
he yelled loudly.

"SHHHHHHHHHHHHHHHHHH, you'll wake . . ."

Just then they heard —

Whooooosshhhh

SPLAT!

CRASH!!

There, in the middle of the room stood a woman who was dripping water on the floor, had flowers poking from her pocket, and wore a straw hat that was big enough to cover Mexico!

"Who... who..... who..... ARE you?" stammered Mollie.
"Where did you come from?"

"Oh, hi you guys! My name is Lily. I used to live in Mexico
until I accidentally got stuck in a blue bottle. Why I tell you
I was trapped in there for more than 200 years," said the
woman while water dripped from her hat.

"But who are YOU two and how did I get out of the bottle?"

"I'm Mollie and this is my brother Max," said the girl.

"I'm sorry but we don't have a blue bottle," whispered Max as he quickly joined his sister on the top bunk. "I just rubbed this piece of blue glass and wished that it was magic."

"Oh Max, that makes me so happy. I think there was JUST enough magic on that little piece of glass to set me free!" exclaimed the smiling Lily.

"I knew those sparkling rocks were special," giggled Mollie.

"And NOW we are going to be rich," Max said with pride.

Lily laughed. "Not so fast you guy. Sea glass won't make you rich. At least not in dollars or cents. But understanding its story will make you very, very wise.

"Why, I tell you, the lesson from this small piece of glass is more valuable than any diamond or ruby. More valuable than any treasure on a pirate ship.

"Want to hear the story?" she asked.

"Of course we do!" they clamored.

Then, without saying a word, Lily swept the big hat off her head. And just like a magician, she pulled a bright green bottle out of the hat!

Lily raised the bottle high over her head and smashed it to the floor. Water and tiny pieces of glass flew everywhere.

The twins were afraid they would never be able to clean up all of the little pieces.

"OH NOOOO!!" whispered Mollie. "This floor is a mess."

"She's right, Lily! We could be in trouble," exclaimed Max in a loud whisper. "Granddad doesn't like noise when he's sleeping or water on the floor. What is he going say about the glass or those little snails?"

"Ohhh, I tell you," laughed Lily, "I will clean this up faster than you can blink your eyes. That cute little crab and those crawling snails will disappear—like magic."

Bending over the mess, Lily grabbed a small chunk of the broken bottle. "See this?" she asked. "This is so sharp it could cut your foot.

"The smooth glass you found today was once as sharp and pointy as the pieces on the floor.

"Your sea glass may have traveled thousands of miles to get here. AND," she giggled, "they could be really, really old. Just like ME!"

"When I lived on the ocean's floor in that blue bottle, I saw a lot of things. I even saw pirates throw ALL of their bottles and trash overboard. Just for fun. Those pesky pirates didn't care one hoot about recycling!" said Lily.

"They threw their trash into the OCEAN?" interrupted Mollie.

"Oh YES!" Lily continued. "A long, LONG, LONG time ago people used rivers, lakes, and the oceans to get rid of their trash. The waves washed it away. They thought it was gone forever.

"So when we find real sea glass we know it started with sharp, pointy edges like the ones here on your bedroom floor."

Max and Mollie both looked puzzled. "But, that's not magic," said Mollie, "that's science."

"Oh, don't you worry. I'm getting to that," laughed Lily.

"You see, the tides, the wind, and the weather keep the ocean's water and things like sea glass moving. It might travel hundreds and hundreds of miles over sand and rocks. The glass might even roll and tumble past old sunken pirate ships.

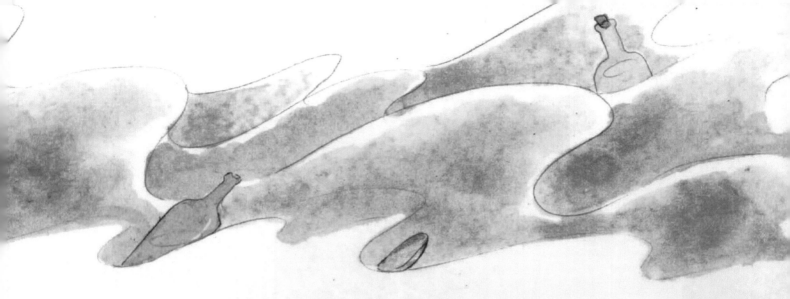

"Even calm waters move the glass

baaaacccckkkkk and
forrrrttttthhhh,

baaaacccckkkkk
and *forrrrttttthhhh,*

Across the sand. For days. For years."

"The waves move like this," Lily said as she threw herself to the floor. Rolling from side to side she said, "When the waves move back and forth, the glass moves back and forth too. With each little movement across the sand, the sharp glass becomes a little bit smoother.

"Eventually, the glass rolls nearer and nearer to a shore where a wave pushes it on to the beach."

"Wow," said Max as Lily groaned and slowly rose to her feet. "Is that why some of the shells I find are smooth?"

"Oh sure. Sometimes the waves are so strong they tumble rocks, shells, glass, trash, and even people," Lily said.

"One time I had a wave tumble me," shared Mollie. "Every time I stood up another wave would knock me back down. I'd just fall down and roll."

"Hey guys we all have lots of tumbles in life," said Lily. "Sometimes things happen that make us feel like we are smashed to smithereens or tumbled like clothes in a dryer.

"We get tumbled when someone bullies us or says unkind things. We get tumbled when something happens that we can't control—like having to move or missing school because we are sick."

Lily sprung into a less than perfect cartwheel and continued the story.

 "There are so many things that can make us feel sad or angry. But, like a piece of sea glass, the tumbles change us and make us stronger.

"Imagine how that small piece of glass has changed since it went into the water," huffed Lily. "Yet, you like it more now. It is stronger and more rounded. Just like the treasures from the ocean change when tumbled, so do we.

"You guys have already had tumbles in life. Max, you had a big one last year."

"I did?" he asked in surprise.

"Remember being picked last for the soccer team?"
asked Lily. "Some of the kids laughed at you. Then you
became embarrassed and started calling them names.

"What happened after that?" she asked.

Max frowned. "I refused to go to practices."

"Then what?" prodded Lily.

"When Granddad found out, he made me go back to the team, PLUS do extra practices," admitted Max.

"And this year?" asked the big-hatted woman.

Smiling, Max replied, "Well—I wasn't picked first, but I wasn't picked last either. Extra practices helped."

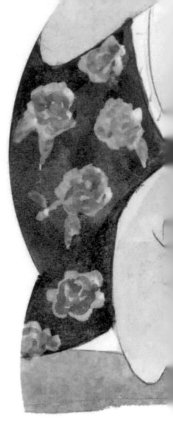

Lily smiled, "Good for you Max. I know those times are hard. But, if we keep trying and keep learning from our mistakes, things WILL get better. Tumbles in life shape who we are and make us stronger.

"Over time sea glass changes and gets stronger. And so... do... we," repeated a very dizzy Lily.

"And that's the end of my story about the magic of sea glass."

As she finished her last clumsy handspring, Max and Mollie climbed down the ladder and looked at each other with a grin. They KNEW they could learn to be stronger, thanks to Lily's silly cartwheels and her story of sea glass.

When they reached the floor, Lily was gone! The room was dry and spotless. No water. No broken glass. No snails.

"Where did she go?" cried Mollie.

They looked everywhere for their new friend. She wasn't under the bed, in the closet, or even in the drawers.

Like magic, Lily had disappeared. The only sign that she had been there was a vase of lilies on the nightstand, more sea glass, and a note:

Dear Max and Mollie,

Thank you guys
for being such
good listeners.
There are lots
of things we can
learn from nature.
Remember the
magic of sea glass.

Love, Lily

Follow up questions for parents and teachers:

1. What kind of special treasures have you found?

2. If you found a tumbled treasure like a shell or piece of sea glass, where would you put it so that you would remember Lily's story?

3. Do you think this story is about finding treasures or something else?

4. When someone hurts your feelings or teases you like they did Max, what would you do?

5. Why do you think Lily says that the story of sea glass is more valuable than pirates' treasure?

Discover Your Own Sea Glass Magic

Searching for sea glass is a pastime and hobby enjoyed by people all around the world. Each piece different; each piece a mystery.

Go online to learn how you can receive — FREE:

- Your very own piece of REAL sea glass,
- Certificate showing where YOUR piece of sea glass was found,
- Collection bag for beach treasures,
- Welcome letter from Lily.

It's easy and it's free. Go to: **www.maxandmolliekidsclub.com**

To purchase additional books, visit **www.maxandmollie.com**